VISIONS

VISIONS

Book Two of The Freak Series

Carol Matas

KEY PORTER BOOKS

Library and Archives Canada Cataloguing in Publication

Matas, Carol, 1949–

    The freak II : visions / Carol Matas.

ISBN-13: 978-1-55263-932-0, ISBN-10: 1-55263-932-0

    I. Title.

PS8576.A7994F743 2007   jC813'.54   C2007-903927-8

The publisher gratefully acknowledges the support of the Canada Council for the Arts and
the Ontario Arts Council for its publishing program. We acknowledge the support of the
Government of Ontario through the Ontario Media Development Corporation's Ontario
Book Initiative.

We acknowledge the financial support of the Government of Canada through the Book
Publishing Industry Development Program (BPIDP) for our publishing activities.

Key Porter Books Limited
Six Adelaide Street East, Tenth Floor
Toronto, Ontario
Canada M5C 1H6

www.keyporter.com

Text design and formatting: Marijke Friesen

Printed and bound in Canada

07 08 09 10 11 5 4 3 2 1

For Per

ONE

WHEN IT'S THIRTY-FIVE DEGREES BELOW ZERO, having psychic powers doesn't help you. Having an extra layer of blubber might. Unfortunately, I have the former, not the latter. And although I should be thinking about my horrible new recurring dream, I can only think about how much longer it'll take me to walk the mile from Kelvin High to Cordova Street. If Ms. Mahon hadn't kept me that extra five minutes after class— grilling me on how I came up with "such an elegant solution" to the math problem she'd given me—I would've caught my bus. Instead, I'm tramping though half a foot of new snow and into a wind that will freeze exposed skin in one minute. None of my skin *is* exposed—I'm not too proud to wear a scarf over my entire face. When Zach came to school a few days ago with a white nose, totally frozen, I decided it was time to stop worrying about how I looked when I went out. No wonder some brainiac finally realized that global warming is not a good name for what's going on in the world. Right now, I'm so cold my teeth aren't even chattering; they're clenched together so hard it hurts. Cold can actually hurt your entire body, I think, feeling very sorry for myself (at this point I'm only halfway home). What good are psychic abilities, anyway, if they don't warn you that your teacher is going to make you miss your bus? Come to think of it, though, I did have a feeling that I should get out of class fast. I ignored it because I was tired and I knew it was going to take me forever to gather up my stuff.

Still, it isn't easy keeping my psychic "gift" a secret. Take math, for instance. I was always good at it. Exceptional, some might say. But now I can almost "see" the answers in my head. Have my skills improved, or is this a new facet of my ability? And then there's the seeing things that aren't physically there and hearing things that aren't being said out loud. Sometimes I can't tell the difference.

Just this morning, I answered Morris when he asked, "Who's going to show up for hockey tonight, in this weather?"

And I said, "Don't worry; everyone'll be there except Finn."

Not only had Morris not said it out loud, no one knew that Finn had gone away except me—and I only knew because I "saw" Finn on the plane and "saw" the others at the practice and "heard" Jason speak when in fact he hadn't! Big groan time, really.

And then shortly after that I let out a giggle when Gerald said he needed to leave school early to go to the doctor because he's got a rash on his butt. That struck me as pretty funny! Of course, he hadn't said that out loud either. He just thought it in big bold letters. If only people wouldn't think so loud! He glared at me as if I knew something—and I did!

I've tried to keep my newfound abilities—apparently developed this past summer when I almost died of meningitis and visited an angel in the astral plane (or whatever you want to call it)—as much a secret as possible. Mom and Dad know, of course, as do my younger brother Marty, my Aunt Janeen, her boyfriend Sahjit, my boyfriend Jon (who happens to be Sahjit's son), Baba, and assorted doctors. None of them seem to think I'm nuts, although I often feel like I am.

I look up to see that I'm almost home. Dreams of hot chocolate are floating in my head. But suddenly they are replaced by images of the dream I've had two nights in a row.

It is night. I am on a street, somewhere downtown, I think, because I can see storefronts and the street lights are on. Snow is falling. It's so cold. I'm not paying attention because I'm rushing to get— I'm not sure where—somewhere warm. Someone grabs me and then I'm not me anymore, I'm them. I have my arms around this person's neck, pulling them backwards, and I draw this woman—the woman I was at the start of the dream— to the ground and look at her face. It's full of terror, and she's trying to scream but her scarf is muffling the sound. I grab the scarf and I pull, and I twist and ...

I am standing still, not a good idea when it's minus thirty-five. And I'm panting. It's so real. Like the dreams I had before the synagogue bombing. As real as that. I sprint the last half block and find the door unlocked, Marty already home. I stand in the foyer for one blissful moment, just letting the heat seep in. Then I begin to take off my mitts, jacket, hat, scarf, and boots. I leave my boots on the rubber mat, throw everything into the hall closet, and head for the kitchen. I yell for Marty, who yells back that he's in the basement, no doubt playing video games. I make two hot chocolates and yell again, this time for him to come up and get his. I grab the peanut butter and some cut up celery sticks that Mom has left in a baggie in the fridge. I stick the celery into the peanut butter jar, scoop a big gob of peanut butter onto it, and chomp down. Best snack ever. I collapse into a chair with a sigh of relief.

The sigh quickly turns into a gasp. I am staring at the front page of the newspaper and on it is the face from my dream, the woman's face. She's been murdered, strangled with her own scarf, sometime around ten last night, on a little side street right downtown. No one saw or heard anything and the police are asking for help.

Marty sits down, takes a sip of his hot chocolate, and grabs a celery stick.

"Hey, Jade," he says, "you look like you've just seen a ghost."

I grimace.

"Really?" His face lights up.

That's Marty. He thinks my powers are cool. He thinks I'm like one of his comic books heroes.

"I saw that woman die. In a dream." I point to the newspaper picture. He leans over, looks at it and tries to appear serious and sad. That lasts about twenty seconds.

"So, you'd better go to the police."

"And what, tell them I dreamt it?"

"Did you see the killer?" He says that last word with relish.

"That's the problem. I didn't. I just saw the victim. And since I had no idea who it was, I couldn't warn her. So what good was the dream?"

Marty shrugs. "Well, it's over now. Don't sweat it."

As callous as that sounds, he's probably right. I had a flash, but there's nothing I can do about it now. I need to focus on my homework, do something normal.

I catch myself. Normal? Yeah, good luck with that.

Like every day you *normally* have a dream that predicts a murder. I sigh and turn the paper over, as if by hiding her face I can wipe out the reality.

"Don't say anything to Mom and Dad," I warn Marty. "They'll just worry."

"No fear," Marty says. And then he starts into a litany of complaints about how boring school is and how it's torture and how he's not going to last the year, et cetera. Marty is the opposite of me. He's just as smart, but he hates studying and school and sitting still and wishes he could play hockey all day—or at least a video game version of hockey.

My mind wanders: Marty thinks I'm cool, and that's nice. Mom and Dad are trying to accept. Jon knows. Aunt Janeen and Baba know and have no trouble with it. But here's the thing. In the past whenever something—anything—happened, my best friend Susie would be the first person I'd turn to. But I still haven't told her any of this. I keep thinking that since it all came on suddenly maybe it'll disappear the same way. I mean, I'm not like those people on television, you know, characters who grew up psychic. It just happened to me out of the blue. One day I woke up and it was there. (I watch those shows, by the way, for research, like they are real, not made up at all.) But I mean, I'm fifteen and up until a few months ago was a science/math whiz egghead. And I liked it that way! This doesn't fit into my plans at all. At all.

TWO

THE QUESTION ABOUT WHETHER OR NOT TO TELL
Susie becomes more than just theoretical much too
soon. Did I have a "feeling" Susie was about to become
an issue? Is that why I started worrying about her in
the first place? Hey, I guess it doesn't really matter.
What does matter is this really bad feeling I'm getting
as I talk to her on the phone.

Dinner is over and Susie and I are doing our usual
after-supper gab, which, I must admit, has become
shorter and less open because right now she's not part
of my secret and Jon is. I end up talking way longer to
him, and enjoying it more because I have someone to
confide in. But Susie can tell that something's different. Sometimes she asks me if everything is okay. She
asks if there's anything about the synagogue bombing I
want to tell her. She tries to assure me she's there for

me. But Susie is the ultimate realist. And so was I—
that's why we are best friends! We'd scoff at the New
Agers in school, the religious nuts, even English
majors! Only science and math and facts were worthy
of respect. And I still totally respect science and math.
I even think there must be some sort of scientific
explanation for all this. But I also know it's as real as an
equation. Susie might not be able to handle it. And I
don't think I could handle her *not* handling it.

Right now she's gushing about this new after-school
job she's gotten tutoring math to junior high kids.
Gordon, a kid in our math class, has a younger brother
who needs help. His parents asked him to recommend
someone and he recommended Susie. Anyway, a few
other parents heard about it and it's turned into a real
job.

So I'm getting this black, black feeling as she talks,
and since she's talking about the new job I have to wonder if the black feeling and the new job are connected.
But what do I say to her? Don't tutor? It's dangerous?
That sounds plain crazy.

"Where is this again?" I ask.

"Harvard Street," she says. "Twice a week after
school."

"Will they drive you home after?"

"You sound like my mom."

"It'll be dark then."

"Yeah. Dark and six o'clock with the streets full of people. You okay?"

Susie and I aren't exactly wimps. We may be eggheads, but we aren't sissies. In fact, Susie does tae kwon do and I've been dancing since I was five. Not that I could knock anyone over with a pirouette or a grand jeté, but I'm pretty strong. This year, because of being sick and everything, I couldn't continue with ballet three times a week, but this term I've signed up for a jazz class on Saturday afternoons and a modern class on Thursdays after school.

"You still there?" Susie asks.

"Sorry, mind wandering."

"Let's meet at The Chocolate Shop after our classes tomorrow," she suggests. She means her tae kwon do and my dance, since tomorrow is Saturday. "Unless you have something on with Jon?"

"Not till tomorrow night—we're going to the movies," I say. "Sure. Let's meet."

"Okay. See you then."

"See you."

I hang up the phone, but the feeling of blackness just gets stronger as I think about Susie. Damn.

I feel kinda like a traitor as I call Jon to get advice. It's always been Susie and me. I should be asking *her* advice. It feels wrong that, now at least, he's closer to me than she is. I explain that to him.

"Everything changes," he says.

Jon's thinking is a mixture of Eastern philosophy and Leonard Cohen.

"You mean she might not always be my best friend?"

"Maybe. It depends."

"It depends on whether I can be honest with her," I sigh.

"You got it."

"I know. I can feel the distance already," I admit.

"Then you have a choice. Either the friendship will just die gradually, or you tell her."

"And it dies quickly."

"You really think she'll dump you?"

"Not exactly. But I'm not sure she'll be able to accept it. It's all so unscientific."

"Maybe you can find a way to describe it to her scientifically," he says.

"Yeah," I say, doubtfully. "Except I haven't figured out a scientific explanation that makes sense to me! I'm sure there are smarter people than me trying to figure this out, but so far I haven't discovered anything—"

He interrupts. "But have you *really* researched this?"

"I guess not so much."

"Maybe it's something you two could do together?"

I grimace. "I don't think she'll be interested. Hard science. That's her thing."

"But your dad is a scientist and he believes you now," Jon says.

"Because after the bombing he had to. It was proof."

"So?" Jon says. "Susie will too, then."

"No, see," I say, "last year Susie did a paper on this skeptic, Garry Pellerman or some name like that ..."

"Yeah," says Jon, "I've seen him on TV. He's always debunking the psychics and alien believers."

"Right! Him. Anyway, she did all this research and thought he was amazing. And then she got a subscription to his magazine— *The Whole Truth*, I think it's called—and she's made that her, well, like, her thing. She's always going on about it and she's taken to calling the English majors goo-goo brains—"

"Goo-goo brains?"

"Yeah, 'cause their brains are goopy."

"Okay. Now I'm a little hurt!"

"Not *you*, of course!"

"No, not me because she knows me. But that's the trouble with 'believers,' right? Now she's a skeptic so she can't accept anything that doesn't fit with being a skeptic. That's why I like English! Nothing is cut and dried—everything is about interpretation."

"That's why I don't like English—usually!" I add, laughing. "Science is so clear and so easy."

"Anyway," he says, "there's no one out there smarter than you. So if this can be explained by science you can do it."

I grin. "You sure know how to make a girl feel like a princess."

I can hear him smiling back.

"How's everything else?" he asks.

I tell him about my dream and the newspaper.

"Okay. That's frackin' spooky."

I smile to myself every time he says that. It's so charmingly geeky. Jon loves *Battlestar Galactica*. Everything is "frackin' this" or "frackin' that." Or, "my gods." I have to admit I'm kind of addicted right now too, especially since watching involves cuddling up all on our own in the rec room, because no one else in the house likes it.

Jon agrees with Marty, though, that there's little to be done about the dreams.

And then, maybe hearing in my voice that I could use a break from this stressful stuff, he asks if I've decided on a movie yet. We argue back and forth between chick flicks and action flicks, him wanting to see the former, me the latter. He loves romantic comedies. I think they are cheesy beyond belief.

Just before we hang up, he asks if I've told my parents about the dream. I tell him I haven't, and ask him not to tell my Aunt Janeen or his dad. I know everyone will just make a huge deal over the whole thing.

It takes us forever to say goodbye but we finally hang up. I do my homework, which includes solving four math problems (something I accomplish in minutes), and then drop off to sleep, hoping for a night filled with dreams of snowflakes and snowmen and skaters gliding over the duck pond at Assiniboine Park. It's a trick Dr. Manuel taught me—thinking good thoughts just before sleep to influence your dreams.

I am walking through the snow. It is so quiet—the kind of quiet you only get right after a deep snowfall. The stars are out and they glitter in the night sky. The snow sparkles in the light of the street lamp. I can see my breath but there is no wind and I can't feel the cold. I just feel how peaceful and how beautiful it is .

I am not on the sidewalk, but am walking on the road, following tire tracks. A man is doing the same on the opposite side of the street. A car slides toward him and he jumps nimbly out of the way before we pass each other.

Without warning, I am jerked backwards off my feet. I am on the ground looking up. But it isn't me on the ground. Suddenly, I am hovering in the air. There's an older woman lying on her back in the street, a look of surprise on her face. She thinks she must have slipped. She doesn't see the form behind her clutching the ends of her scarf. Holding them in the air ...

I wake with a start. I am sitting in my own bed, dripping in sweat. I can still see her face so clearly.

Should I call the police? And say what? Look for an older lady somewhere. It might not even be in this city. It might not even be real. But what if it is?

THREE

I WAKE UP BEFORE THE ALARM GOES OFF, STUMBLE downstairs and turn on the television in the kitchen. No news about another murder. That's good, right? Mom is gulping down her coffee and Dad has already left to run some errands. Marty is still asleep.

"Uh, Mom?"

She holds her cup suspended in mid-air and stares at me. Mom's not a psychologist for nothing. She can tell just from the tone of my voice that something's up. Funnily enough, she's having a harder time accepting my "powers" than Dad. I proved my ability once with the synagogue bombing and that was enough for him, but Mom still can't seem to wrap her head around it. Plus, I know she worries more. She doesn't want me to get into trouble or to have to deal with ugliness. She wants me to be dating, to have fun, to be a normal teenager. That word again: normal. Gotta love it.

"I'm dreaming," I say.

She puts her cup down and waits.

"The woman that was killed? Did you see the paper?"

She nods.

I force myself to continue because I don't know how to handle all of this. I need help. I can't make this decision on my own. Of course, only last night I'd made Jon promise not to tell anyone, but that was before I'd had another nightmare.

"I dreamed her death. I saw her face. I saw her being strangled. But I didn't see the killer." I pause. "And last night I dreamed that someone else was killed the same way. Should I call the police?"

"You're sure it was the same face, the same woman? Are you *positive*?"

I nod, yes.

"And did you see where the next attack would happen? When?"

I shake my head, no.

"The police are likely already considering that it might happen again," she answers. "They'll be checking with her family and friends, of course, but they'll also be thinking about the worst-case scenario, a serial killer. And you really can't offer them any more than that."

"Unless," I say, suddenly getting an idea, "they get a sketch artist to draw the face and they could publicize it! Then if friends or family or even the woman saw the sketch maybe she could be saved."

"If they believed you," she says.

"If they believe me."

"If they don't think you're responsible," she adds.

I stare at her. Of course, that's the worry. When you go to the police with information, will they think you have an inside track? I was right about the bomb, but I couldn't tell the police exactly what was going to happen beforehand, only that *something* was going to. Besides, only a few people in authority knew about my "premonition." I mean, we didn't want to make a big deal out of it in case the press heard and I really became a freak for everyone to harass. So, we'd pretty much be starting over now trying to explain things to them.

"But what if this thing is going to happen tonight?" I say.

"Then it's already too late. Even if they believe you, a sketch artist wouldn't have a picture before tomorrow.

Waiting a few hours won't hurt. We have to think about this." She takes a big gulp of coffee. "Go to dance class. Maybe the best thing would be for dad and me to talk to the police without you. Remember I did that consulting for Detective King a few years ago? I could call him. It's Saturday, but he might be in, especially with a murder that needs solving."

I grabbed some cereal and milk and poured myself some juice. "Okay," I agreed. Really, what else was there to do? After all, I'd spilled the beans so the decision didn't have to be all mine, and now I could let Mom run with it. "Susie and I are meeting after class. I'm going to try to tell her."

Mom's eyebrows go up. "Everything?"

"Yup."

"She may surprise you," Mom says.

It won't be long before I find out.

~

Dance class is fun, if exhausting. Just a few months of not doing anything and I find I'm in pretty terrible shape. Still, I'm able to follow the routine better than anyone in the class, so Madame Lorette places me in the front row, centre, after only about ten minutes.

And because of that I really push myself. I'm soaked through by the time we're done. Thankfully, they now have showers in the change room.

I get to The Chocolate Shop a few minutes before Susie and plop down in a booth. Right beside me, a psychic is giving readings to two middle-aged women.

He's a young guy, maybe mid-twenties. He has a bright glow around him—almost like he's lit up. He's shuffling cards but suddenly he looks up at me. He stares for a moment, then winks and goes back to his cards. I watch him as he lays them out and talks softly to one of the women. Her friend is writing down everything he says. I try to catch what he's saying and almost jump out of my seat when Susie plops down across from me and says, "Hi!"

"Hi," I answer back, dragging my eyes away. "Sorry, didn't see you there."

"That's because you were trying so hard to eavesdrop," she says. "Not polite," she adds.

"Yeah, right," I say. Then I have a thought. "Maybe we should get a reading," I suggest.

She snorts. "Come on. It's all smoke and mirrors. They check your body language; they get you to give away clues so they can make good guesses. And anyway," she adds, "I'm broke."

This isn't starting well.

"What if it isn't fake?" I counter. "Maybe there's something to it. Come on, I'll pay for mine—if he's good, I'll treat you, too."

When our waitress comes to take our orders, though, she tells us that each reading is twenty dollars.

I had been assuming five. Twenty is well out of my league.

Susie gives me "that" look, meaning see, they're all charlatans.

I think about what Jon said—I could lose Susie either way. At least this way she has a choice. She can choose to be my friend, no matter what, or she can choose to dump me. I take a deep breath. Just before I speak I hear a voice.

"Go for it, girl."

I look around. The psychic sitting across the aisle from us is staring right at me. He grins. Man, he must be good. But on the other hand, why is he reading my thoughts? I didn't ask him to. 'Course, no one asks me to, either, and I do it without meaning to all the time. Can't say I like the feeling, though.

"What *is* your problem?" Susie says, sounding really annoyed.

I look back at her, shocked. Susie never talks to me

like that. But it does have one effect. It makes it easier for me to tell her.

"My problem is that I'm worried about how you're going to react to what I'm about to tell you."

"Huh?"

"You asked what my problem was."

"No," she says slowly, "I was *thinking* that. I didn't say it out loud."

I put my head in my hands. Then I have to laugh. "Right. Well, that's my problem."

I look up. She's giving me a "she's gone crazy" look.

The waitress arrives with our order. We're silent until she leaves.

I glance at the guy in the booth. He's still talking but his glow has faded. I look at one of the women. She's sick, I can tell. So can he. He's trying to tell her.

I take a deep breath and plunge ahead. "Here's the deal. You know all that weird stuff that was happening when I got back to school—guessing Jason's girlfriend was gonna dump him and Zach's marks and all that?"

She nods.

"It was like, I could …it's so hard to describe …but I could 'hear' them thinking." I pause. Then I look right at her. "I could hear their thoughts. I could even see the future. Like, really. No joke."

.

She grins. "So what am I thinking?"

"Good one, Jade."

She looks puzzled. "Did I just say that?"

"No."

She frowns.

"And now you feel hurt. You think I'm scamming you. You think maybe I'm trying to pick a fight."

"I don't! I just. . . . What *is* this?"

"See, the thing is . . . the thing is," and again I have to pause and work up the courage to keep going, "I'm *psychic*. Really. I can see things. And I was the one who found the bomb—"

"*You* were?"

"Because I kept dreaming about it. And now I'm having more dreams."

"Okay, okay," she says. "Hold on. You'd better start at the beginning. Let's look at this in order."

That's Susie. Order. Logic.

If only. So I try.

FOUR

Susie has one question on her mind. it's practically shouting at me, which means she doesn't need to say it.

"You want to know why I didn't tell you any of this. You want to know if we're still best friends. You wonder if you should even still *be* my best friend."

She shakes her head as if to clear it, but that won't help.

"I didn't want to accept it," I say, searching for a way to explain. "I kept hoping it would go away and I'd never have to tell you. I mean, let's face it, you aren't exactly Miss New Age. You think all of this psychic stuff is ridiculous. And since you got into the skeptic thing, well, you've closed your mind to even considering that any of this could be true. I never wanted to have this conversation. I didn't want to hear my best

31

friend tell me I'm nuts, a freak. I didn't think I could stand it."

"I'd never call you a freak. Never."

"But you'd *think* it," I say. "You couldn't help it."

She stares at me for a minute.

Then comes the question I'm *really* dreading.

"Who else knows?"

I tell her.

"Jon knows?"

I nod.

"You told him and not me?"

"I *had* to. Jon was directly involved. His father's life was in danger." I tell her the story about Sahjit and the car and how that led to Jon and me investigating the dreams.

"That's why you two are so tight. He's the one you've been confiding in," she says when I finish.

I take a sip of my hot chocolate. It's cold. The pie and the gelato we each ordered sits uneaten. Susie starts to play with her melted gelato, pushing it around on the plate and making patterns out of it. "So all those weird things that kept happening at school were because of this?"

"Yes."

"Because you believe you are psychic." She flattens

the apple pie with her fork and mixes it in with the gelato.

"Yes," I say, trying to hold down the growing feeling of irritation. "That's what I just said, isn't it?"

"Well, forgive me if I don't jump for joy here," she snaps back. "My supposed best friend has hidden this big secret from me, while totally confiding in her boyfriend. And besides that, if she had bothered to confide in me maybe I could have helped her see how, how …"

"How ridiculous it all is?" I finish the sentence for her.

"Yes!" she says defiantly. "Exactly. That's what friends are for. Unlike boyfriends, who will tell you whatever you want to hear."

"That's not fair! Jon found it hard to believe too! But because of me his dad wasn't hurt."

"Something else you didn't tell me about."

She continues to mash her food. I can feel her brain working overtime. She's trying to sort everything out into some logical explanation that will not only fit, but will convince me as well.

"Look," I continue, "I pretty much knew you wouldn't believe me, but I'm telling you all this now because, firstly, you know how much your friendship means to me and I need to be straight with you, and secondly," I stop for a second to try to pick my words, "I have a funny feeling about this job of yours. I don't know what it is exactly. Right now it's just a dark feeling. See, the trouble is, I get these feelings, except half the time I don't know what they mean. Like, I could have a bad feeling 'cause you're going to catch a cold, or I could have a bad feeling 'cause something really terrible is going to happen. I see this blackness, but I don't know why."

My phone rings, startling both of us. It's my mom.

"Are you guys still at The Chocolate Shop?"

I look at my watch. It's past six.

"Oh man," I say, showing my watch to Susie. She pulls out her cell and calls her parents.

"Yeah, we're still here," I tell mom.

"Okay. Dad'll come get you. He'll be there in ten or so."

"Thanks. Did you talk to Detective King?"

"Yes."

"And?"

"He says he can't spend the money on such a long shot. But you should describe her to me, I'll write it down, email it to him, and if something else happens and you keep having dreams they'll have you in next time."

"Doesn't do this lady much good," I say.

"I know, but it all sounds so out there to him. I was surprised he even suggested this."

"What lady?" Susie asks.

Great. How am I going to explain *this*?

I am saved having to answer her though, because I glance up to find the resident psychic standing at our table.

"You don't really believe this can be happening, do you?" he says to Susie.

"Excuse me?" Susie sounds none too friendly.

"May I?" He's asking to sit with us.

"Sure," I say, scooting over in the booth.

He sits beside me, but he's looking at Susie. And she's glaring at me for inviting him to sit down.

"There's something dark coming to you," he says to her, without preamble. "I know your friend here has already told you. I just want you to listen to her. She's the real deal."

I can almost hear Susie thinking that he and I have somehow planned this. I am about to tell her that, really, truly, I've never met him before when he looks at me and says, "Hey, you'll get used to it. It's not so bad. And not all psychics end up giving readings at twenty dollars a pop. You can still be a scientist. Maybe you can help figure it out."

"That's what my boyfriend said to me," I say, and then realize he has just tuned in to my wanting to be a scientist without knowing anything about me.

"They say if you hear something three times from three different sources it's a message, a real message, from the universe," he tells me.

"Well, that makes two," I say.

"So, I hate to be a drag here," Susie interrupts, "but does it bother anyone that both of you are seeing some horrible, dreadful crap in my future?"

"Sorry," we both say at the same time.

The guy takes out a card and gives one to Susie, one to me. "That's my number. I can't ask you for your phone numbers—it'd look a bit off, right? Call me in a few days. I'll tell you if I get anything clearer."

The card reads, John Smith. Psychic. Hah. Talk about a normal name for a not-so-normal kind of guy.

He gets up and goes to his booth, where more customers have settled in.

We gather our gear, pay our bill, and wait at the door for Dad.

"Hey girls," he says, as we get into the car, me in front, Susie in back. "How's it going?"

"Is this all true?" Susie says to him as we start to drive.

"You told her?" he asks me.

"Yep."

"It's all true," he confirms.

"But how?" she says.

"That we don't know," he answers.

There's a silence.

"But Jade could sure use her best friend right about now," he adds.

More silence.

Dad turns on the radio. I try to hold back the tears. Have I just lost my best friend?

FIVE

THE MOVIE JON AND I GO TO IS ALL ABOUT changing the future. We had agreed on science fiction/ action as a compromise. After, we go to the coffee shop in the same mall as the theatre—that way we don't have to go outside again until it's time to go home. There's a band of university kids playing Celtic music. I try to talk loud enough so Jon can hear me but quietly enough so no one else can.

"I mean, I see the future," I say, "and I know it *can* be changed because I've done that, too. So, is there really such a thing as fate? And if there is, what is it?"

"Maybe you were always *meant* to change the future, which means it was fated all along," Jon says. "I was reading this book the other day"—half of the sentences Jon utters start that way—"about how we have no free will at all, we just think we do. We're totally genetically conditioned to react to certain things in certain ways, and that, along with our upbringing, leaves little room for actual real choice. We choose things sort of automatically, *believing* we are making our own choices."

I think about this for a minute. "At synagogue a few weeks ago, the rabbi gave a sermon about the Ten Commandments. He pointed out that all except two begin with 'Thou shalt not,' instead of 'thou shalt.' He said something similar to your book. He said that humans are likely to do things without really thinking, so we need to be told *not* to do things." I stop to think for a moment. "No free will? That kinda sucks."

I take a huge bite of my samosa and for a moment I don't care about anything except the delicious taste of the food in my mouth.

"You must be having the dreams for a reason," Jon says.

"What? I'm some kind of divine instrument?"

He smiles. When he smiles I really couldn't care less about any of this.

"Who knows?"

I make a face.

"If you don't like that explanation, maybe it's something less cosmic—your own brain reaching out there, picking up on all this, showing you things. My dad says we all have our own purpose in life, but we can express it in many ways. For instance, your mom likes to help people, so she becomes a psychologist. She could have helped people by doing other jobs, right? A teacher, a volunteer …Maybe she chose psychology because it fit a deep inner longing to do something she connects with and honours. And you can express your talents in many ways too—not just concrete math and science. Maybe, although we don't understand it yet, what you are seeing is somehow related to equations and physics and all that stuff."

I continue to munch on my samosa, wondering how I ever ended up with such a deep boyfriend—and thinking that he's too cool for words. Other girls have to sit and listen to how their guys won at hockey or curling or something. I get to listen to this. Then I realize he's waiting for me to say something back.

"So I need to find out what my inner purpose is, and not worry so much about how I end up expressing it?"

"Maybe."

"Do you know what yours is? Your purpose?"

He smiles again. "I'm too young to have that figured out."

"I'm too young, too!" I protest, and a small bit of food falls out of my mouth and onto my plate as I speak. Gross.

"Sorry." I think I'm blushing.

"I didn't see a thing," he assures me.

He is perfect, isn't he?

"Did you know your Aunt Janeen and my dad are thinking of moving in together?" he asks, changing the subject.

"Shut up!" I pause. "How would you feel about that?"

Jon's mom died of cancer when he was only ten.

"I think it would be great. David leaves home next year to go to university down east. And I'll be home only a few more years. Ben could use a mom. And they're crazy about each other."

"Who? Your dad and Aunt Janeen?"

"No, Ben and Janeen. And my dad, too," he adds.

"Hey," I say, "I just had a thought—Aunt Janeen isn't that old; she's thirty-three. You could have a little sister or another brother one day."

"That would be cool," he says.

We talk about that and school and regular things and by the time I get home I feel normal again. I seem to be able to turn off my overactive senses when I'm with Jon. But just like with everything else, I don't know why. Maybe we're already so much on the same wavelength it just doesn't kick in. Who knows?

Anyway, I fall asleep feeling happy and relaxed. But that doesn't last long. I'm awake at around four. The same dream. The same woman.

How much fun is it to watch someone being strangled over and over again? I'm not sure how much sleep I get after that, but it's not much. The image stays burned in my brain.

I do manage to stay in bed longer than usual, and stagger down to the living room around ten. I am flopped in front of the television in the living room watching cartoons—about all my little brain can handle—when Mom wanders in.

"Another dream?" she asks.

"Same one," I answer.

She sits at the desk in the corner and opens her email.

"Describe it," she says.

I try to remember every detail—the colour of the scarf (red), the coat (black), the hat (black), and boots (black). I also add a description of the street. Mom types it all into a message and sends it off to Detective King.

"So," she says," what are you up to today?"

"Susie and I were supposed to go skating at the Duck Pond, but ..."

"But?"

"She was totally freaked out yesterday."

"Well, maybe you need to prove it to her, like you did with me and dad."

I look at her. "Sometimes you have some decent ideas."

"Well, thank you. High praise indeed!"

I call Susie and pretty much bully her into going skating. Her mom drives over and picks me up. But even that feels weird. The dark cloud that I've been seeing around Susie is also around her Mom. Great! What does *that* mean? I guess that whatever is bad for Susie is going to be bad for her mom, or make her mom sad, or something.

Once at the rink, we realize we aren't going to last long. It's warmed up a bit—to minus twenty—but the wind is biting. We put our skates on in the shelter and head out. There are only a few other hardy souls.

"Tomorrow I'll prove it to you," I say.

"How?"

"I'll read people. You choose who. Then you ask them if I'm right. Without letting on what I'm doing."

"Okay," she agrees. "Can we drop it till then?"

"Fine with me."

After fifteen minutes we give up, call for a ride, and go home.

I just hope I can perform on demand tomorrow. I need to convince Susie this is real. Because she has to listen to me—something bad *is* coming.

SIX

Not only is it minus thirty when I wake up, but my throat feels like it's on fire. Maybe braving the weather yesterday wasn't such a great idea. Ordinarily, a sore throat combined with horrible weather would be the perfect combination to keep me snuggled up in bed all day, but today I decide not to tell Mom I'm sick. I need to show up at school so I can convince Susie.

I have the bus schedule timed down to the last second. The bus stop is right on Grosvenor, and we're only a few houses down the street. I time it so that I spend only a few miserable moments outside—covered from nose to toes, of course. Today, once on board, I don't even mind cramming up against the unruly hordes. At least they provide some extra warmth. I mean, two minutes outside and I already feel like a popsicle.

When the bus reaches Kelvin everyone tumbles off like a piñata bursting, except this piñata is filled with hormones covered with parkas and toques. The din seems louder than normal to me, maybe because I'm feeling sicker by the second. I think I might have a fever.

I noticed Susie getting on the bus at Ash, but she was too far away for us to talk. She waits for me, though, and we scurry up the school steps together.

"Are *you* feeling okay?" I ask.

"Yeah, why?"

"I've caught something. My throat feels like it's burning up and when I swallow it's like gulping down cut glass."

"Charming. Why didn't you stay home?"

"I wanted to do this."

"Okay," she says, as we get into the deliciously warm entranceway, "how's it going to work?"

As I rip off my scarf, she adds, "You don't look that great."

"Thanks. Well, let's conduct our experiment and then maybe I'll go home early." We head for our lockers. "Choose someone."

She points at Jason who is walking toward his locker, near us. I focus on him, and get—nothing.

"That's weird," I mutter. "Choose someone else."

She points at Matilda.

I stare at her and get the same: nothing.

It's as if there's a fog around everyone. Usually thoughts pop out at me in blasting colours, or I can hear them loud and clear. Sometimes, I can see things around people. And it's not like I want to or anything, I can't help it. And now that I want to ...

I put a hand on my locker to steady myself. I feel dizzy. After months of having other people's thoughts and feelings bombarding me all the time, this silence is more than a little odd. Have my psychic powers gone away as suddenly as they arrived? I figured if that ever happened I'd be thrilled, but now I feel funny. Kind of lost.

"Sorry," I say to Susie. "I'm not getting anything. It's weird."

Susie shrugs. "Hey, don't sweat it. I didn't expect—"

Then she bites her tongue, but it's too late. I know she was going to say that she didn't think it was real anyhow.

"Why don't you go to the nurse and get something for your throat?"

Actually I have some painkillers in my bag. I take a couple and grab a water bottle from the stash I keep in my locker. Halfway through English I'm starting to feel better and begin to concentrate on the lesson. We're studying *The Tempest*. Magic. Prospero gets so caught up in his magic that he loses sight of his responsibilities and lets his kingdom go to rack and ruin. And he's so blindly obsessive he lets his brother take advantage of him when he should have had the upper hand, considering his superior abilities. Just goes to show you, I think, that having an ability—any kind of ability—is neither good nor bad. It's all in how you use it. Maybe I've been concentrating so hard on my new-found abilities I've forgotten about my old ones: logic, clear thinking, all that.

I'm not quite sure where this train of thought is leading but I'm interrupted by Sarah nudging me.

"Hey?"

I look up. Everyone is staring at me. Mr. Crossley has obviously asked me a question.

"Could you repeat that?" I ask.

"Why do you think Prospero ended up on the island?" he says. "For the *third* time, Jade."

Well, I guess my powers aren't all gone. I simply repeat what I'd just been thinking.

"Excellent," he says, looking a bit surprised. English isn't my strongest subject. But I do like Shakespeare.

You can really get into him in a way you can't with some books that are so boring you could scream.

"Balance," Mr. Crossley says. "That's very good, Jade. Prospero has lost his balance. And as the play goes on and we see him immersed in the island and nature, we again see the theme of balance in everything and how important it is."

As my fever goes down because of the drugs, and my sore throat becomes bearable, the fog begins to lift. Suddenly my brain is crowded with noise—people's thoughts—and the colours return. I can see people's auras, and in a room filled with colour, there's Susie surrounded by black. A shiver goes down my spine.

By the time we get out into the hall the chaos that is my life has returned. I'm half relieved, half sickened. It would be so much easier without all of it. I catch myself. If that's really true, why did I feel so worried about losing it? This ability is not my identity. It's not me. Yeah, keep telling yourself that, Jade, I say to myself.

Laura, a pretty good friend of ours from class, is leaning against the lockers. She has a blank look on her face. And suddenly, I know why.

"Ask Laura if her mom is all right," I say to Susie. "There's something wrong—maybe a lump in her breast."

"I can't ask her that!" Susie says.

"Do you want me to prove this to you or not?"

Susie sighs. She goes up to Laura. I go with her.

"Hey, Laura."

Laura starts. "Oh. Hey."

"Everything okay?"

"Sure."

"You look kinda worried."

"Me? No."

She starts walking away.

I glare at Susie. She glares back. Then she blurts it out. "Your mom—is she alright?"

Laura stops and turns around. "Who told you?"

Susie grasps for an answer. "Not sure."

"She's going for a biopsy today," Laura says.

"She's going to be fine, I promise," I say.

And she will. I see light all around her mom. Nothing bad is going to happen.

Laura smiles wanly. "Thanks." She wanders off.

"That was weird," Susie says.

I shrug. "That was nothing. I mean, compared to the dreams I can't figure out. One more?" I ask.

Susie nods.

We keep going down the hall, heading for science class.

I spot Mollie. She has a huge bright light around her—pure happiness. I can "see" her kissing Brian. "Here's a good one," I say to Susie. "Come on."

I walk up to Mollie. "So, you and Brian, eh?"

Someone slams a locker. I see Rachel, her face dark with anger. Uh oh.

"You and Brian?" Rachel repeats.

Mollie looks at me in horror, then at Rachel.

"Rach, we didn't … I mean … you guys were gonna break up, right? I mean …"

"You, you—" Rachel looks like she's going to hit Mollie, but she just turns and walks away, tears flowing.

"Nice one, Jade," Mollie says. "Just let me know if I can ever return the favour."

"I'm so sorry," I say, following her down the hall. "I didn't know it was a secret."

"Yeah, well, only me and Brian knew, so it's obvious who shot his big mouth off. I'm gonna kill him!"

"No, really, it wasn't him. I—I saw you."

"You liar. We were at my house! How could you have seen us!"

Mollie lives in the granola belt across the bridge, nowhere near me, or Rachel, for that matter.

She stalks off.

Susie stares at me. "It is real."

"I know."

"Wow. It's real," she repeats.

"Yeah," I say, "And you can see how popular it makes me."

"Hey," says Susie, "if they were cheating they deserve all the misery they are about to get." She grins. "It's kinda funny."

And my heart feels light as feather. My best friend believes me. I'm not alone at school anymore! I throw my arms around her and give her a big hug.

And then it sinks in. If I can't figure out why Susie is surrounded by blackness, I might soon be alone. Very alone.

SEVEN

It's not till I get home that I see the newspaper. I'm feeling worse again; the drugs have worn off and the cold is moving from my throat into my head. I start sneezing and can't stop. Through runny eyes and masses of snot, I stare at the picture on the front page.

No question, it's the woman from my dreams. She was found strangled with her own scarf on a small side street near the university. The police are now strongly hinting that they think the two murders were committed by the same person. This woman had no enemies. She was a grandmother of five.

I'm still staring at the paper when Mom comes home. Marty is at Jamie's house and Dad is picking him up later.

I slide the paper over to Mom as she sits down at the kitchen table. She looks at it for a minute, takes a deep breath, then reaches for the phone.

"Aren't you even going to ask me if it's the woman in my dream?" I say.

"If it wasn't, you would have told me," she says.

I nod.

She calls Detective King. "She's not looking too well right now—bad cold," Mom says, after listening for a moment. "Nine? Sure. We'll be there."

"He wants to see us at nine tomorrow," she says, putting down the phone.

"Do they know when she was killed?"

Mom skims the story in the paper. "Between eight and nine at night."

It had snowed late in the day yesterday. That would account for the fresh snowfall I saw in my dream.

"At least I have an alibi," I say with a nervous laugh.

"Yes, considering we were all watching *The Matrix* for the millionth time," Mom says.

The Matrix has suddenly become my favourite old movie. Reality. What the heck is it, anyway? I mean, the movie is so interesting because all those people think they are living in reality and nothing can convince them otherwise, but they aren't. And is our world the same in some way? Is there an unseen universe out there that I've only caught bits and pieces of? Is this material world the illusion?

After *The Matrix*, we watched an old episode of *X-Files*. And then I talked to Jon before going to sleep, as always.

"You'd better go to bed," Mom says. "I'll bring you up some soup."

"Can I lie on the couch in the basement?" I ask.

"Sure."

Television is bad in the afternoon, but with a head as full as mine reading is out. I find some cartoons, but before I know it I'm asleep.

When I wake up the house is quiet. I stagger upstairs. It's past nine. I've slept for hours. Mom and Dad are reading in the living room.

"How are you?" Mom asks.

I groan something. Mom gets up. "I'll make you some chicken soup."

She always has batches of chicken soup in the freezer ready for such emergencies. Soon I'm sitting at the table gulping it down, along with a soft drink and toasted challa. The perfect food for when you're sick.

Dad sits with me while I eat.

"I hear your dreams are coming true again," he says.

"Lucky me," I reply.

"I'm sorry, Jade. This must be tough."

"No, it's loads of fun, seeing innocent people getting killed over and over." I know I sound like I'm feeling sorry for myself, but I am!

"Worse for them, though," Dad says.

That's true.

"Might be better," he says, "if you can think less about how it's affecting you and more about why you're getting the dreams. Use your logical mind."

I look up from slurping my soup. "I was thinking something like that today in class."

"I always feel better if I can do something about a problem," Dad says.

"That's the trouble, though," I say. "I see the victims, but nothing that could give me any clues or warnings."

"Not true," Dad says, "you see their faces."

"That hasn't helped, has it?"

"What if you could describe the next woman—if there is one, and let's hope there isn't—and the police could announce that they need to speak to this person, maybe for help with their inquiries? That way, they could publish her picture and maybe stop it."

Mom has been listening to all of this as she stands at the counter cleaning up.

"I think that's a good idea. I'll suggest it to Detective King tomorrow."

"It's better than nothing," I agree, "but it doesn't help catch the guy."

Dad shrugs. "You can only do your best."

He kisses me on the forehead. Mom gives me some cold medicine to help me sleep and I go upstairs to take a hot shower. The steam helps my nose clear out a bit.

I call Jon, tell him I'm sick and that we'll talk tomorrow. I don't tell him about the police because the drugs are already taking effect. I'm out almost as soon as I hang up the phone.

I sleep the sleep of those drugged with cold medicine, blissfully unaware of any dreams. Mom has to shake me awake in the morning. She feels my forehead.

"Fever's gone," she declares.

"I feel better." I'm still groggy, but the sore throat is gone and I've stopped sneezing.

I eat some toast, drink a whole mug of tea with honey, and take another cold tablet. Then we set off.

Marty is very impressed that I'm going to help the police.

"Don't tell anyone," I caution him. "People will think it's weird, not cool."

"Yeah, yeah," he says, as he heads off. He's dying to get some celebrity out of all of this, but there's no way I'm going to let him.

"Good luck," Dad calls after us.

Mom and I drive downtown, a pretty harrowing trip since it's so cold that the exhaust from the cars is creating a fog. You can hardly see a foot in front of you. We park in the Public Safety Building parking lot and make our way up to Detective King's office. He's actually waiting for us by the elevators and takes us to his little cubicle. Ah, the glamour of police work.

Detective King is probably in his mid-thirties, with a shock of black hair and almost black eyes. He's medium height and stocky and may have eaten a doughnut or two in his life. He has a round face and a straight nose and a nice smile, which he tries out on me as we walk.

It's a little forced and I can tell he's not sure exactly what he's dealing with here.

He motions us into two chairs and he sits behind his desk.

"You're trying to decide if I'm crazy or the real deal or a suspect," I blurt out as I take a seat. "My Mom'll tell you I was home the night before last watching videos. Sometimes I think I'm crazy, but apparently according to Dr. Manuel, my shrink, I'm not. You have my permission to call him, though, and ask. So that leaves the real deal. You wouldn't be feeling so grumpy if your car had started this morning. But it didn't, and you had to call someone for a lift. She talked your ear off and put you in a bad mood. But at least you heard all the office gossip and more on the ride in from Charleswood."

He just looks at me, his eyebrows going up a bit.

"What does this someone look like?" he asks.

"Red hair," I answer.

He nods and then looks at Mom. "That's a little unsettling."

She smiles wanly.

"My dad had this idea," I continue, doing that talk a mile a minute thing I do when I'm nervous, "that you could publish a sketch of the next person I dream of if it happens again and maybe that way we could save her."

He thinks for a minute and then says, "Save her and maybe not save someone else."

"Huh?"

"That might work," he says, "if the killer is targeting specific people for a specific reason. But, if he's choosing at random, then if we warn off one person, won't he just choose another? And then ..." He stops.

"And then," Mom jumps in, "Jade might feel responsible for the other person."

"Exactly."

The enormity of that idea hits me. Right. I save one woman and by doing that, doom someone else. My interfering would actually cause the second fatality.

"But if I see her and I do nothing, and we don't know if there will be a second attack, won't I be responsible for the first one?" I ask.

He shrugs. "I can't answer that."

Oh, great. A lose-lose situation for me. But as I'm about to sink into being really, really depressed, Dad's words come back to me. Don't think about you, think about them. Do something. Think. Use your brain.

"Will you be warning people in general to be careful?" I ask.

"Yes. We're going to have to. We don't want to start a panic but we're going to warn women not to walk alone at night."

"Then if I see another woman I think we should publish her picture. What if she comes forward and from her work or her habits or the people she knows you can connect something with the other two? It at least gives you a start, right?"

"Right," he says, nodding his approval. "It's what I'd like to do. I just wanted you to know the consequences."

"I understand," I say. "But maybe this won't happen again."

"And what are the chances of that?" he asks.

I stop for a minute to think. "Almost none," I answer. "I feel like right now there is nothing stopping this guy."

Detective King leans back in his chair. "That's what our profiler is saying, too."

"So we should get back in touch if Jade has any more dreams?" Mom says.

"Yes. And if you could just sign a statement saying that you were with her the other night, and the time before."

Mom doesn't get mad. She knows they need to rule me out, and so far it's not as bad as either of us thought it might be. She does that, we all shake hands, and she and I find our own way out.

As we walk past all the cubicles filled with police I am inundated with images. I can practically see a guy who is being interviewed shooting up in some dark cold alley; I see one officer looking at a file and around him are images of knives and blood; I see another looking through photos and I know they are of young children that have been horribly abused. I have to turn away. What a way to spend your life. But as I focus on individual policemen or women I can feel a sort of wall between them and all of the negative vibes. They've learned how to keep them at a distance. Maybe one day I'll be able to do the same.

EIGHT

MOM DECIDES TO LET ME SKIP SCHOOL FOR THE rest of the day. I crawl into bed and go back to sleep. In the afternoon, I go down to the basement and watch TV until I hear footsteps. Susie crashes down the steps into the rec room.

She's carrying a stack of books in her arms as well as various papers and printouts. There is a gleam in her eye. She plops all the books on the coffee table, almost spilling my cola, and declares, "We are going to figure this out!"

I burst out laughing. Man, it's good to have her back on my side.

I glance through the books. Two are psychics' memoirs, two are science books, and one is by Deepak Chopra. I pick it up.

"Yeah, I've read part of that already." Susie says. "He talks a lot about reality. He says——"

I interrupt her. "I saw him on the *Late Show* one night last week."

"Right! He says the way we envision the world is the way the world turns out. And that after we die, we keep creating. And that there are no coincidences. And that . . . well, he doesn't really seem to believe in the kind of God that is personal, you know? It's more like we are all creating creation. I don't know," she continues, "I just skimmed it. So I might have it all wrong."

"But it's not so much about being psychic, is it?"

"Not directly." she says. "This one is way more like that." She holds up one of the memoirs. "But," she adds, "getting back to Chopra. It's not about being psychic, per se, but it *is* about the unseen world. He says we are all part of the same thing—some call it a unified field. There is no such thing as body versus mind. There is body/mind all as one, and that body/mind is one with the universe, because the atoms and sub-atomic particles that flow in and out of us are the same ones that flow in and out of everything else. We're breathing in particles that could have been part of an ocean in India, or a dog in Russia or, like, our most favourite movie star! Did you know that the body replaces almost all of its atoms every year? So when we see ourselves as fixed, solid, it's wrong, an illusion. We're energy! And that brings us to thoughts. Chopra thinks thoughts are real, just like this table. If I think a thought, a good one, it'll have force. So will a negative one. Thoughts are just another form of energy."

"So," I say, picking up on the idea, "if someone is thinking a thought, and that thought is real, then I'm just scanning it. I see the thought the same way you see this table."

"Exactly!" she says. "It's not really so weird, when you think that, like, dogs can pick up scents we can't and hear things we can't. Does that mean when we are walking on a street the scents aren't there? No. They are there. We just can't smell them. And maybe that's what you do. Thoughts are real. It's just that most people can't see them. You can."

"When Chopra was on TV," I add, "he asked what happens when a person at home turns off the TV? The program they are watching would still be there, right? But the person at home couldn't see it or verify it. It's the same thing."

"Do you, do you ..." Susie stops.

"What?"

"See dead people?"

I grin. "No. Not yet. But maybe I will. I'm just starting after all."

"The thing is, if you can see dead people, well, that means something, right?"

I know exactly what she's getting at. Both of us used to believe that there was no God, nothing but logic and science. Since "dying" during the whole meningitis thing and seeing Zaida, I've had to reconsider all that. But I'm still unsure about what it means. I haven't become all religious, that's for sure. But I just don't know any more and I think about it a lot.

"It kind of shook me up that way," I admit, explaining what happened when I was sick.

"After it happened, I asked everyone what they believed in. My Baba *knows* there's an afterlife and God and she believes that everything is *B'shert*, meant to happen. And Aunt Janeen thinks our souls are infinite and we reincarnate and we decide our future in between lives. And Jon believes in karma—action. When you act, the action is burned into your memory and if it's bad you have to burn it off—if not in this life, in another."

"Wow. You have been looking into it," Susie says.

"It shook me pretty badly," I admit. "I was all about science. Now I wonder."

"There has to be a way to mix the two. Maybe we just need to find out what it is," she suggests.

"Number three," I mutter.

"What?"

"If you hear something three times it's a message from beyond—wherever that is," I add. "Remember, that guy at The Chocolate Shop said something just like that?"

"Right," she says. "I do."

She hands me an article she cut out from the paper. "See, here's a guy from Toronto that says that the universe didn't result from one big bang. He thinks it was a big bounce."

"A bounce?"

"Yeah."

I start to read.

"And this matters because …?"

"Because," says Susie, "if we're part of an infinite universe that's always contracting and expanding, everything *is* based on science. Math. Geometry. See? The article says the creation of the world is not based on faith like the big bang theory—you know, the universe exploded from a single entity. By the way, it was a priest who first thought of that theory. This bounce theory is based on science. Our stuff. And oh, oh—" she gets excited here, "see, if it's based on science then we could meld that with quantum physics and string theory and that brings in the idea of parallel universes and Chopra talks about our brain being like, well, a radio. Our brains are just receivers, but our minds are universal."

"What? Wait, slow down," I say. "What's that about our brains?"

"Yeah. What if there is, like, this universal consciousness and our brain just filters it for us?

"So you mean I'm tapping into that? Now that's interesting. Where did you read that?"

"I'm not sure." Susie starts to flip through the books. The phone rings.

I pick it up.

"Hello, sweetheart. How are you?"

"Baba!"

"I haven't heard a peep from any of you in days," she says. Baba is the best guilt tripper in the universe.

"I'm sorry," I say. "I got sick and, well, I'm having dreams again."

"I called to tell you not to walk alone. I've been reading online about the ... did you say dreams?"

Baba is wintering in Palm Springs, like she does every year. She's a snowbird.

"Yes."

"What about?"

"The murders."

"Oh, you poor thing!"

Suddenly tears well up in my eyes. I feel sorry for myself all over again.

"Now, anytime you want to come out and stay with me you know you can, right?"

"Right."

"Is Mom home?"

"I don't think so. I'll go check." I take the phone upstairs. Marty is in the kitchen with his friend Doug eating pizza pops. No sign of Mom and Dad.

"No Baba, she's not home yet."

"Zaida is a little worried about you. That's why I called. You be careful with all of this."

"What did he say?"

"Just that." Of course, Zaida is dead, but Baba swears she talks to him all the time.

"I promise. I told Susie about my 'powers.'"

"How did that go?"

"A little rough at first, but now it's great."

"Good for you. Tell Mom to call me."

"I will, Baba."

"Love you, sweetheart."

"Love you, too."

I hang up and grab a couple of fresh drinks for Susie and me before returning to the basement. As I walk down the stairs and see Susie sitting on the couch the blackness surrounding her is so intense I almost drop the drinks.

"You okay?" she asks me.

"Yeah." I stop. "It's just ... I don't know ... what use is this 'ability' if I can't figure out how to use it? I'm so frustrated!"

I don't want to scare her to death by talking about this dark cloud, but I know something is wrong. "I mean, I get these images, colours, but I don't know what they mean."

"Are you talking about my dark cloud?" she asks.

"Maybe."

She thinks for a moment. "We need to be logical. Maybe you can't figure it out because you haven't had enough practice," she suggests. "Maybe you need to go to some sort of school."

"A school for psychics?"

She giggles. "Where everyone knows what's about to happen." She pauses. "There could be something in these books," she suggests.

We start to flip through them again, especially the

two memoirs.

"Let's try an experiment," Susie suggests after a few minutes of reading. "It says here that this psychic meditates and 'quiets' her mind. So let's try to be quiet, breathe deeply. Maybe if we're both in a quiet space you can read me better."

We both sit and start breathing. Unfortunately, it just feels silly and we end up giggling.

Just then, Doug and Marty run downstairs and tell us they want to play video games.

"Let's go up to my room," I suggest. "It'll be quieter."

We take our drinks and head upstairs. I shut the door and we sit cross-legged on my bed.

We both close our eyes and take lots of deep breaths. I don't suppose this is how you meditate correctly but we need to start somewhere. As I become calmer, images do start to float into my head. I see a dark street. I see a room full of kids. I see Detective King. I see Susie's mom. Again I see the room, and this time Susie is there with the kids. And I get a bad feeling— the dark cloud seems to be hovering over all of them.

I open my eyes.

"It's your tutoring!"

"What?" Susie opens her eyes.

"This feeling . . . It's something about your tutoring. I don't know what. But you have to promise not to walk home alone."

She looks a bit green.

"I promise," she says. "So, it worked?"

"I think it did! I got more than I had before. I saw a group and you teaching them. It's connected somehow."

"Great," she sighs. "This is pretty spooky."

"You're telling me," I say.

Shortly after that, her mom comes to pick her up, and a little while later, Jon calls.

"I need you to teach me how to meditate," I tell him without preamble.

"Sure," he says easily. "We can do it this weekend. It's not hard. Well, it is hard, but it's simple to teach."

I tell him about Susie and what I saw and the police.

"I hope there aren't any more dreams," he says, "for your sake."

"Me too."

But that, as my Baba says, isn't meant to be. Not long after I fall asleep another dream comes to me.

I am walking. It's so cold I'm almost shaking. I'm heading to my car. And then something pulls me from behind. I am looking at myself from up above. My skin is dark, my black

*hair cut short, no hat. A small mole on my right cheek, dark
brown eyes, opened wide in shock ...*

I wake up, drag myself over to my desk, flip on the
light, and write down everything I can remember. I'll
need to tell the police.

And then what?

NINE

FIRST THING IN THE MORNING, MOM TAKES ME down to the police station, where I read my notes from the night before to a sketch artist. She asks me questions and we work on the sketch until it looks almost identical to the woman I saw in my dream. Detective King tells us that it'll be in both papers tomorrow and on all four local newscasts tonight. Hopefully, the woman will see herself, or someone close to her will notice. Then she can go to the police station and they'll warn her.

I dread going to sleep tonight. Will I see her again? Or will I see someone else? Will my interfering just create a new victim?

After the police station, Mom drops me at school. As I walk up the steps, I realize that I'm much better physically. I'm still feeling the effects of the cold, but not as much. And Jon called to say he could get the car tonight so he'd come over after supper and teach me a meditation technique.

Susie's first tutoring class is this afternoon and I'm determined to go. When I'll have time for all the homework I've missed over the last few days, I have no clue. Me, who's never missed an assignment unless I was too sick to do it! Well, as Mom says, there's a first time for everything.

Susie, however, is not at all keen on my going with her.

"It's my gig," she objects as we walk down the hall to math.

"I know, but maybe when I'm there in person I'll 'see' something. Get a clearer message."

"I don't know," she says, unconvinced.

"I do," I say, trying to convince her. "I'll stop bugging you. That's got to be worth it, all by itself."

"I guess," she admits. "In that case, you might as well help me. There are four kids. Let's take two each. It'll be good for them to be in smaller groups."

"I won't take any of your money," I assure her.

"Okay," she agrees. "That seals it."

Math class is almost embarrassing. I've done none of the homework but I'm able to give the answers almost off the top of my head. Afterwards Ms. Mahon asks me to stay.

"Jade," she says, "your ability seems to have reached a whole new level." She waits before continuing, hoping for an explanation.

"I guess," I mutter.

"I was thinking that perhaps you'd like to move up a grade and take grade 11 advanced math with Mr. Chesney?"

"Really?"

"Really. I've already asked him and he says it'll be fine. Talk to your parents. Your dad is a math professor, isn't he?"

"Yes."

"Well, you come by it naturally then."

I burst out laughing.

She looks at me. "I'm not sure I get the joke."

"No, it's nothing," I say. *Sure,* I want to say. *I come by it naturally from Dad and supernaturally courtesy of who knows what!*

"Does it matter that we're already halfway through the year, though?" I ask.

"Here are the textbooks," she says, handing me the algebra and geometry texts. "Have a look through the first half and see if any of it makes sense to you. Also, next year you really should take my physics class. I think you'd find that pretty interesting."

Oh man, am I going to turn into a math prodigy on top of everything else?

"Thanks, Ms. Mahon," I say. And lugging the two heavy books on top of my others, I go find my fellow eggheads for lunch.

Patti and Jason are sitting with Susie as usual, and Morris and Leah are also there. It's true we're the eggheads, but somehow we're not considered geeks and losers. Not sure why. Mom says it's because Susie and I are two of the prettiest girls in school. Sadly, that could be the reason. Shallow though it is, I'm thankful for it. No one wants to be the kid everyone avoids.

I got a taste of that when I came back to school in the fall and started blurting out everything I "saw" and "heard." I was getting a major rep for being weird. But I've worked hard to keep a low profile over the last few months. It's amazing how fast you become a two-second wonder. Everyone forgot about me as soon as Libby Desroches got caught doing hard-core drugs in the locker room before volleyball practice. Libby— leader of the team that was going all the way to the championships. Oh, and after that, Lewis Bradley got in a fight in the hall with a couple of seriously deranged gangsters and ended up in the ICU for two days. That wiped me off the map totally. Thank you, bullies everywhere.

I plop down at the cafeteria table. Not known for missing much, Susie spots the Grade 11 texts right away. "No way!" she says. "They're accelerating you?"

"Maybe."

"Do it!" says Jason. "Then by Grade 12, while the rest of us are slaving away, you'll have one less course to take."

He has a point. And it would be more interesting. And Dad could help me.

"I might," I say.

"Do you *feel* it's a good idea?" Susie asks.

I glare at her. I know what she means, but I don't need her drawing attention to my little gift. Plus, the thing is, I seem to be the last person who knows what'll happen to me. I can look at her and get feelings but I can't seem to look at myself. Although, I guess that's not totally true. How many times have small things happened, and I've just had a gut feeling—like, let's not go to this restaurant and then when we get there it's so crowded we can't get in. Stupid stuff like that. The thing is, I'm usually right. Actually, I was always a little bit like that—even before I almost died and my gut feelings turned into full-blown whatever it is I have now!

Morris leans back in his chair and says, "Geometry. I'm taking simple math next year. And I'll be lucky to get through that."

We ignore him. He's gonna be drafted by the NHL before he's out of high school, so simple math will be all he'll need. He'll have someone to take care of his million-dollar-plus salary.

I see Patti looking at him surreptitiously. She likes Morris but doesn't think she's good enough for him. She goes for jerks who boss her around and shout and intimidate her. Still, Morris is dangerous in a different way—no one messes with him on the ice and it somehow carries through in life, even though I've never heard him raise his voice to anyone. Maybe they'd be a good match. She's supersmart. Not at math or anything in particular, just smart and creative. I suddenly get a vision of her starring in a movie and before I can stop myself blurt out, "Hey Patti, have you thought of trying out for the school play?"

"No," she says.

"You should," I say. "There's a perfect part for you."

Susie raises her eyebrows. "Yeah," she says, "you should. Come on, we'll go see when the audition is." She glances at me as she pulls Patti out of the cafeteria. Oh, Susie. All action. Maybe she trusts my ability too much!

Still, I see Morris gazing after Patti. And I can almost hear him thinking, *An actress? That's kinda cool. And she's pretty. Wonder why I never noticed?*

I can't help smiling to myself. Moments like this make me feel like Wonder Woman.

That good feeling manages to stick with me through the afternoon. Even on the way to Susie's tutoring gig I feel optimistic. Maybe this black cloud thing is just some stupid glitch, like she's going to get sick with a bad cold, or the tutoring gig will be too much work and she'll have to quit. I mean, not everything has to be life and death, right?

I keep trying to tell myself that as I walk into the basement. Mr. and Mrs. Lawrence have set up a small classroom with a table, chairs, notebooks, et cetera.

There are four kids already waiting for Susie. Mrs. Lawrence introduces them to us after Susie introduces me and explains that I'm just here to help her get started and to diagnose the problems. All four kids are in grade eight and having trouble. Dad always says that most math trouble just comes down to bad teaching and that it's rare to find someone who simply can't do the work.

Four faces look up at us. Mindy is a tiny girl, only around five foot one, pretty, with curly black hair and big brown eyes. She's got a copy of a Philip Roth book open in front of her, so I can see right away she's a good reader and probably just doesn't "get" math.

Next to her is Justine, a plain face with long brown hair, brown eyes—she looks bored and miserable. She hates school, I can tell right away. Next is Bob, a tall, lanky kid, also looking slightly bored, with blond hair falling over his face and pale blue eyes, not giving away much of anything. I can't seem to get a read on him. Finally, there's Chase—the Lawrence's younger son—he's got a cellphone and he's texting someone under the table. He's cute. Yeah. He just wants to have some fun, and for him, fun does not happen at school.

Susie assigns me the two girls. We sit down and I give them a couple easy problems and watch them try to solve them. Right away I can see where they are running into trouble. I explain it to them in a way I think they should be able to connect to and they do. It's kind of fun and before I know it it's time to leave.

All four look surprised when Susie's mom walks down the stairs and says, "Sue, I've been waiting for ten minutes." I don't think they thought they'd ever understand a math problem. Ever.

Susie's mom had insisted on picking us up since no one is taking a chance with walking after dark. I'm hoping that my worries about Susie will become clearer to me now that I've been to a tutoring session, but no such luck. In fact, the opposite happens. Both Susie and her mom seem wrapped in a black cloud that's denser than ever.

"So?" Susie asks quietly as we are driving to my house.

"Nothing," I say.

"Never mind," she says. "You tried. Talk later?"

I tell her I'll call her and get out of the car. As I watch it drive away the bad feeling gets even worse.

I kick at some snow in frustration and then go inside. Maybe Jon can teach me how to connect with this super consciousness or collective unconscious or greater mind or whatever it is we're all connected to. Hopefully, the answers to all my questions are there. They certainly don't seem to be anywhere in my little pea brain.

TEN

Jon and I are sitting cross-legged on the floor in the rec room, having shooed Marty upstairs and away from his precious video games. Thank goodness for the thick carpet Mom put down here a couple of years ago. I am trying to breathe. Okay, now I'm giggling. It just seems so silly—focusing on your breathing—but that's all Jon is having me do. The idea is that you let your thoughts tumble around, bringing your mind back to your breathing until your thoughts go away, or quiet down. Basically, Susie and I were on the right track the other day. It's not working, though.

"Let's try adding a sound," Jon suggests.

"What, like *oooohm*?" I say. I've seen that in the movies.

"That. Or any sound. Is there a Hebrew word you like?"

87

"I like *ain sof*. It means 'the infinite, no end.'"

He smiles. "I like that. I'll try it, too. So just focus on that word; say it once on your breath in, once on your breath out. Breathe slowly, in through the nose, out through the mouth."

I try that. It works much better. I can feel myself calming down. My mind seems to almost empty, and all I can hear is my own thoughts saying "*ain sof*" over and over and over … And then, suddenly—

I am walking in a large parking lot. It is brightly lit, but deserted. I'm thinking about my last shift and how the baby co-operated and came just before I had to leave. I smile to myself. A gorgeous fat boy, eight pounds four ounces, first boy after two girls, parents so happy.

I feel something tug on my scarf. I hadn't heard anything. I try to turn but I'm pulled backwards and fall hard on my back, hitting my head on the concrete. The impact is so strong that I'm too stunned to move. And then I'm not me. I'm hovering over me, looking down, and I see a face. It's not my face, it's … it's … it's … Mrs. Norman! It's Susie's mom! And someone is pulling on her scarf, pulling, she can't call out, she's choking …

My eyes fly open. Jon is sitting in front of me—eyes closed, a calm, happy look on his face.

"Jon." My voice is a whisper.

He opens his eyes. "What is it?"

Tears well up in my eyes.

He scrambles over to me and takes me in his arms, holding me close. I cling to him, sobbing now. He tries to soothe me and finally the tears start to dry up, replaced by a cold dread in my heart. I pull away.

"It's Susie. The black cloud—it's not her," I stammer out. "It's her mother."

Just then Mom comes down the stairs.

"Jade!" she exclaims. "Detective King just called. They found her! The woman saw the picture, went into the police at around five and they've warned her and—"

"And she's not in danger anymore," I state. "Someone else is."

"You don't know that," Mom objects.

"Yes," I contradict her, "I do. I just saw the new victim."

"Well, we'll just do the same thing," Mom says.

"We don't need to."

"Why?"

"Because it's Mrs. Norman."

"What?" Mom sits down on the chair by the couch.

"That's what I saw. It explains why I keep seeing this black cloud around Susie. It's not her that's in danger. It's her mom."

"Did you see where?" Mom asks.

I nod. "In a parking lot. She was thinking about work so it's probably in the hospital parking lot."

Mom brightens. "But that's good! You saw where. All she has to do is avoid that, right? She doesn't have to drive there, does she?"

"Oh my God!" I exclaim. "What if she's there now?"

I grab the phone and dial Susie's number. No answer.

"I'll call the hospital," Mom says. She hurries upstairs to look up the number.

Jon tells me it's going to be all right, but I don't think it is.

Why don't I get to see the murderer? Why don't I see something that could really help?

My mind is racing. Nurses work twelve-hour shifts. Mrs. Norman just picked us up, so logically she's either just started a shift or this "vision" is about something that will happen in the future. I mean, it can't be happening now because she was thinking about something that had happened after a long shift.

But what if Mrs. Norman picked us up on her dinner

break? I mean, she's worried about Susie walking home alone so she leaves work, skips dinner, picks us up ... But she could have asked Mom. Except she's so independent, she *never* asks for help with anything ...

Jon and I follow Mom upstairs and find her and Dad talking. Dad turns to me. "They can't find Mrs. Norman. They're so busy down there. We can't seem to make them understand that this is important. I'm going to drive down to the hospital."

"Can I come?" I ask.

"Yes."

Jon wants to go as well. We throw on our winter gear and head out to the garage. The cold hits my nostrils and they immediately freeze up and stick together. The car isn't as bad, though. Thank goodness Dad had plugged in the heater. We start the drive to the hospital—it's only about ten or fifteen minutes away when the traffic isn't heavy.

I'm in the front with Dad, who asks me to go over the vision I had while meditating. Mom spilled the whole thing to him so quickly he missed half of it.

I go through it again, and when I'm finished, he says something surprising. "So, the future isn't fixed then."

"Dad," I exclaim, "can we have a theoretical discussion some other time?"

"But it's not theoretical," he insists. "It's important. It means that, just like with the bomb, if you can see something clearly enough, you can stop it. Because that other woman is no longer in danger. If she were, you would have dreamed about her over and over again, the way you did with the women who died. But you didn't. That woman's future has changed. And you changed it."

"Yeah, that's great," I say. "I mean, I'm glad she's okay, but how do I live with myself if something happens to Mrs. Norman?" I try to hold back a sob. "My best friend in the whole world will have her mother murdered, and it will be because of me!"

"No," Dad says firmly. "That's not going to happen. We're going to stop that from happening."

"And if we do," I say, "then what? What other poor mom or sister or daughter will be next? It's like I'm playing God or something. I should never have gotten involved! I should have stayed out of it."

"Jade," Dad says, "you can't think like that! You need to do the right thing for the right reason, even if the outcome is bad. And we don't know yet what the outcome will be. We don't know if what you did will make things better or worse. But you knew a woman was going to die and you tried to stop it. That's all you could do."

"And," Jon adds from the back seat, "you don't know how everything fits in the grand scheme. Something that looks just terrible in the moment can be good in the end, and something that looks great in the moment can end up being a catastrophe. I mean, look at your dreams about the bombing. You thought *they* were a catastrophe and made you weird. But you saved my dad because of them."

"You can only take things one step at a time," Dad repeats, "doing the best you can. You can't control the universe. You can't."

I try to take in what he and Jon have said. Are they just trying to make me feel better? It doesn't seem that way. And I can't really argue with their logic, although I feel like arguing. I *want* to be able to control the universe. And right now, it seems as if I'm some sort of pawn in a very nasty chess game that universe is playing against me.

ELEVEN

We rush up to the maternity ward but a nurse at a large desk stops us from going in.

"It's very urgent that we see Mrs. Norman," Dad says.

"She's with a patient."

"This can't wait," Dad insists.

The nurse looks down the hall and sees another nurse coming toward us. "Cathy," she calls, "Marjorie is in room 3C. Can you take over for her for a few minutes? These people need to see her."

Cathy nods and turns back down the hall. We wait for what feels like hours but must be only a few minutes. Finally Mrs. Norman appears. A huge sigh of relief escapes me.

"Is Susie all right?" she says, as she hurries over to us. "What's happened?"

"It's not Susie," Dad says. "She's fine. Is there somewhere we can talk?"

"Is it Neal?"

That's Susie's dad. He's a pilot and is away a lot on long-distance routes.

"No, no," Dad says, "no one is hurt."

"But they said it was urgent."

"Is there somewhere we can talk?"

Mrs. Norman leads us into the maternity lounge. There are no people in it, only a TV and some chairs. It's nice and quiet.

"Marjorie," Dad says, "can we sit for a moment?"

I can see he's desperately trying to find a way to tell her. I can't stand it.

"Look," I say, "I told Susie, and at first she didn't believe me. You know how sensible she is, right?"

"Right," Mrs. Norman says slowly, looking at me like I've gone off the deep end.

"But now she *does* believe me because I proved it to her, and I need you to believe me, too."

She looks at my dad. He shrugs.

"Well, Jade," she says, "I'll try."

I've always liked Mrs. Norman, although she's so efficient and good at everything she scares me. I mean, she cooks, she remodels the house, she bakes these amazing cakes and cookies, all while holding down a full-time job. Susie takes after her, of course.

I continue. I can't worry about how nutty this must sound; I just have to plough ahead. "After I almost died I developed these psychic abilities and now I've been dreaming about these women who are being attacked and ... I just had ... it wasn't a dream, it was more like a vision, and ... it was *you*. I saw you being attacked in the parking lot here."

Mrs. Norman just stares at me. She doesn't say anything. Then she looks at my dad. He nods, as if to say it's true. She looks at Jon, and he nods too. She looks back at me.

"Are you sure?" she says.

"It was you," I say. "I dreamed the others too, but I couldn't warn them because I didn't know who they were or even, at first, if the dreams were real. But, of course, I recognized you right away."

"I won't go to my car alone," she says. Just like that. No arguing, no freaking out, no questions. "And thank you, Jade." She actually gets up, and gives me a hug. "Now I'd better get back. Can we talk about this tomorrow?" She is saying this to Dad.

"Absolutely."

"Maybe you'd better tell security to warn all the people going to the parking lot," she says to Dad.

"Of course!" he exclaims. "I should have thought of that."

"What if they don't believe you?" I say. "What are you going to tell them?"

"I'll have them call Detective King," Dad says.

We go into the lobby where we can use our cells and Dad calls Mom. She's very relieved to hear that we've found Mrs. Norman. She promises to call Detective King right away. She has his cell number too, in case he's off work already.

I try to call Susie again once we're in the car. She answers right away this time. For a second, I have no idea how to tell her.

"Hey, what's up?"

"Susie, we're just coming home from the hospital."

"Oh my God, what's happened?"

"Nothing! I mean, no one's hurt. It's just, I had another dream—well, a vision, actually, because I was awake. You know, Jon and I were meditating and, and …" I stop, desperately trying to find a way to tell her.

Jon leans over from the back seat. "It's fine. You

stopped it. Tell her."

"Here's the thing," I continue, "I saw your mom in this vision."

"And?" she says.

"Your mom was the next victim."

There's a dreadful silence that seems to go on forever. Then she asks, "Is she alright?"

I'm an idiot. Why didn't I tell her that first? "She's fine! We've just come from the hospital. She's promised not to go into the parking lot alone. She's fine."

There's a silence. Then, "Why her?" Susie asks.

I pause. "I have no idea."

"You didn't see him."

"No."

"You're on your way home?"

"Me and Dad and Jon."

"Can you and Jon come over? Dad'll be back around midnight. I'm gonna stay up and tell him and get him to pick up mom."

I turn back to Jon. "Can we drive over to Susie's for a bit?"

"Sure," he answers.

"Dad?"

"Yes, but I want you back no later than ten."

When we get home we check in with Mom to make sure she got hold of Detective King. She did and he's going to have security all around the hospital.

Then Jon and I drive over to Susie's, only about two minutes away by car.

She lets us in and we head for the kitchen. In her usual always-doing-something way, she's made us both hot chocolate—very welcome and soothing.

We sip as we sit around the kitchen table.

"Why my mom?" Susie asks again.

"I don't know."

"But maybe there's a reason," Susie says.

"None of the others seem to be related in any way," I say. "It must just be random."

"Wait a minute," Susie says, actually putting up her hand like a traffic warden. "How can we be sure it's random? Think about it. We're best friends. You start having these dreams, which are actually warnings. And at the same time you see this dark, like, cloud around me."

"Huh?" I say, not quite following her train of thought.

"Wait." She pauses for a minute and then asks, "Why did these dreams start?"

"How should I know?" I exclaim in frustration.

"They just started and they proved to be true, right?"

"Right. But, *why*? You say it's random. But my mom, *your best friend's mom,* ends up being one of the targets. So what I'm saying is that, logically, there must be a reason. And maybe my mom *is* the reason. Maybe somehow you are personally connected to this because of my mom."

"But your mom only became the target when the other woman was warned. Otherwise that other woman would have been next," I object.

Now it's Susie's turn to say, "Huh?"

I realize that I haven't had a chance to explain what Detective King predicted, so I tell her.

"Oh, I get it," says Susie. "You're assuming that if that woman had been the next victim my mom would never have been in danger. That it's all random. What if it *isn't*? What if my mom was the intended target all along?"

"And the other women were what then?" I ask. "Just practice?"

"No, of course not! But just because we don't know the why of the other women doesn't mean there isn't a why about my mom. A reason."

"So you're saying that I'm connected to this in some way. But how?"

Jon looks at Susie. "This never occurred to me. She could be right, Jade. We should definitely consider this."

"Never occurred to me either," I grunt, feeling both a little stupid and a little angry that it hadn't. But when I stop to think about it, the dreams and the dark cloud around Susie and her mom both started at around the same time. I assumed they were separate; why wouldn't I? But what if Susie is right?

"There's only one way we'll know for sure," Jon says.

"What's that?"

"If you have another vision and it's of another woman then this whole thing must be random. The other victims were accosted in the street. Maybe the murderer was going to happen on Mrs. Norman just accidentally in the parking lot. But if you have another dream, and if it's Susie's mom again, even *after* she isn't attacked in the parking lot, then maybe the murderer has fixated on her and is sticking with her. And then for sure it's more than purely random."

"This is crazy," Susie says. "Now I'm going to be nervous until your next dream!"

"What if I don't dream anything, though?" I say. "What if something happens and I don't get a warning this time? It's not like I can arrange these things."

Jon takes my hand. "Then you aren't meant to see it."

I wish I could believe that. I can tell by the look on Susie's face that she doesn't feel quite so laid-back about the whole thing either. I can see she's about to say something snarky to Jon, but she bites her tongue. I wouldn't blame her. That was a little insensitive—I mean, it is her mom, after all. And for sure he wasn't that fatalistic when we were talking about his dad a few months ago.

"That wasn't what I meant," he says into the silence. "Sorry Susie, that must have sounded stupid. I just meant that Jade can't control all this and she shouldn't put too much pressure on herself."

"Yeah, I get it," Susie sighs. "You're forgiven. And anyway, Mom is safe now." She gets up and gives me a hug. "Thanks," she says.

"You're welcome," I say. "I guess sometimes this ability doesn't suck."

Jon drives me home not long after. I'm beat.

He walks me to the door and gives me a very sweet kiss goodnight. I go in and am barely out of my boots and coat when Mom appears.

"They've caught him!"

"What?"

"Detective King called. A guy tried to grab a nurse by her scarf on William Avenue. There was all that security around the hospital because of your warning. She managed to scream and a policeman caught him before he hurt her. He's been taken down to the Public Safety Building."

I walk into the kitchen and sit.

"I can't believe it," I say.

"Me either."

"It's over?"

"It's over!"

"Who is it?"

"Some guy on drugs. He's been in and out of jail for years. A bit crazy. Well-known to the police."

"And they're sure it's him?"

"They're sure."

I call Susie and tell her. She's beyond relieved. Then I stagger upstairs. I'm so tired I can barely stand. I run a hot bath with bubbles, and soak because I'm still cold from being out so much tonight. The temperature is minus thirty-six right now.

The heat slowly seeps into me. I relax. Is that really it, then? I sink under the bubbles, relief washing over me.

I finally get out when Marty starts pounding on the door. I'm in bed and asleep in minutes.

The sun is bright on my eyes, so bright I can hardly see. The snow is sparkling and even though the sun is shining there are small flurries. But they come down like a million diamonds, landing on the front yards, sparkling and shimmering like a picture book fantasyland. I am hurrying from the car port at the back of the house to the back door, arms full of groceries. And then I'm pulled from behind. I fall on the path, my head hitting so hard I can't think. And then I'm looking down and I see it's not me, it's Mrs. Norman. She looks so surprised. And her scarf is being pulled, tight, tighter . . .

I sit up in bed gasping. Then I yell.

"Mom! Dad!

Both run into my bedroom.

"What is it?" says Mom.

"The guy they caught isn't the guy. It's not over."

TWELVE

Somehow I manage to fall back to sleep after telling Mom and Dad, but I wake up in the morning with a sinking feeling. After all, the police think they've caught the guy, right? So who's going to believe that Mrs. Norman is still in danger?

I call Susie before I even get out of bed.

"Susie?"

She can hear in my voice that something's wrong.

"Don't tell me you had another dream?"

"Yeah."

"About?"

"Your mom again."

"But they've caught the guy, right? Maybe you're just having an old-fashioned, regular nightmare."

"What if I'm not?"

"You mean they have the wrong guy?"

"Well, it wouldn't be the first time that ever happened."

"So you think my mom's still in danger?"

"The dream felt the same as the others. If it was a nightmare I think it would have been more like a nightmare and less like a vision. I mean, I don't know for sure. How could I?"

"So the where and when of the attack might change but not the how," Susie states.

"I guess. You'd better tell her."

"I will, but I can imagine what she'll say. I mean, I don't know how much of this she believes in the first place, and now the police have caught someone . . . you fill in the blanks."

"I get it. She won't want to know. But if I'm dreaming about her there has to be a reason, right? Isn't that what we decided? So what's the reason? Is there a connection between her and this guy, or me and this guy, or you and this guy—something that is tying us all together?"

"How are you going to figure that out?"

"No clue."

There's a pause. "See you soon."

"Yup."

Visions

We meet up as usual on the bus. Susie squeezes her way down toward me.

"Could this suck any worse?" she says.

"No. How did your mom take it when you told her?"

"She doesn't really want to believe it. But I told her the whole story from the beginning. She doesn't know what to make of it, but she thinks it's probably just a normal anxiety dream. The police have the guy and that's that."

The bus lurches to a stop and we tumble out with the rest of the mob.

"Yeah," I say, "maybe she's right. That would be great."

"But what if she *isn't* right?" asks Susie. "And she's still in danger?"

As Susie says that, the dark cloud surrounds her again. I sigh as we climb the steps. No use mentioning it now. What good would that do?

The day passes somehow. I try to put everything out of my mind and just concentrate on my work.

After school, I catch the bus for my modern dance class downtown. Dad is going to pick me up after. As I'm getting changed a card falls out of my bag. John

Smith. And a phrase reverberates: "There are no coincidences."

I grab my cell, call Dad and ask if he can pick me up at The Chocolate Shop at six, instead of at the dance school at five-thirty. It's only a short walk, and the street will be busy so he says I can go.

I find this class easier than the jazz, as the technique is much more like the classical ballet I'm used to. But I'm still exhausted when it's over. And I can feel that I'm a little rundown from what's left of my cold. I shower, change and hurry over to The Chocolate Shop. And there's John, not even giving a reading, just sitting there. He recognizes me and waves. I go over to his booth.

"Have a seat," he says, smiling.

"Thanks."

"I had a feeling I'd see you again."

I smile back.

"You have a question."

I tell him as concisely as I can what's been happening. He listens, not saying a word. When I finish I add, "Here's the thing. It's not good enough seeing the victims. I need to find out who the murderer is."

"You're sure he's not been caught?"

"I hope he has. But the dream last night felt just as real as the others, and I still see black around Susie."

He pushes his tarot deck to the centre of the table. "These help me focus," he explains. "Cut the deck in half." I do. "Now shuffle." I do. He lays out the cards. And then he starts to talk, kind of quickly, in quite a different tone of voice.

"I see a wall—a silence, an anger so deep that there's no motion around it. No waves, no energy, no clues for anyone. And I see numbers, like equations. They are everywhere, covering you, sinking into you. I feel danger, too, not only for your friend and her mom, but for you as well."

He stops and looks up at me. "That's it. That's all I'm getting. I'm not sure what it means."

"Thank you," I say. Then something occurs to me. "I should pay you! Oh no, I never thought . . . and I have no money!"

He smiles. "I don't want you to pay me. But if you'd like me to give you some tarot lessons you can pay me for that."

"Really?"

"Sure. I think you might be able to use the cards as a tool for focusing your talent. There are lots of decks though, and there are different cards. There are even Jewish Kabbalah cards. You'll have to sift through the decks and see which one calls out to you." Then he stops, pauses for a minute and says, "Wait a minute. You're going to Palm Springs."

"I am?"

"Yes. And there'll be a conference of some kind there. You should sign up. You could learn a lot. As long as . . ."

He stops himself.

"As long as I'm still breathing." I finish his thought.

He nods.

"What do you do when you see bad news in the cards?" I ask him.

"I warn people," he says. "I need to. I'm always honest. I can't control events. Somehow, I can just see them."

"How do you do it?"

He thinks for a moment. "My theory is that there is no past, no present, no future. It's all one. And I tap into that larger time/space and sometimes can pull things out." He pauses. "I know the burden you're carrying right now is a heavy one. And you didn't ask for it. Few of us do. But you can't ignore it. A gift, an ability, a curse—whatever you call it, and I've called it all of those, you need to deal with it. The more you learn about it, the more you'll be able to integrate it into your life instead of letting it rule your life."

"Have you done that?" I ask.

"I have," he says. "And I must say, I'm pretty happy. But my talents are nothing compared to yours. I can feel you're very special."

I grimace. Yeah, it's great to be special. "Do you, like, channel dead people?" I ask.

"Sometimes," he answers. "Sometimes it's more like reading thoughts. I can sort of 'hear' what's going to happen or is happening, sometimes I see it, like a TV show. And sometimes spirits do seem to come through."

He pauses. "Your grandfather has passed, correct?"

"Yes!"

"He calls you his ... his little, like, diamond, or sapphire. I see gemstones."

"Yes! Jewel. My name's Jade!"

"He says it's not over. It's ... he can see a number, and your friend is involved, involved. He keeps saying involved."

"Why doesn't he just tell me the killer's name?" I exclaim.

"Wait." John concentrates. He sits very still. "I'm getting a jumble of things. Young kids. Numbers. He probably *is* trying to tell me the name—I just can't 'hear' it."

I write down everything he's told me and then, horrified, notice my watch. It's five past six and Dad must be parked outside illegally. I throw on my coat and grab my bag as I thank John over and over.

"Be careful," he says to me.

"I will!"

I leg it to the car. Dad's being relentlessly honked at. I get in, buckle up, and tell him what's just happened as we drive off and the honking stops. My head is so full of thoughts I feel like it's spinning.

"List the things he told you," Dad suggests.

"Susie is involved. Young kids. Numbers." I pause. "Oh my God."

"What?"

"Her tutoring! Numbers. Susie. Young kids. And John saw someone cut off, sort of hard to read. And," now the words are tumbling over one another, "and there was this one kid—I couldn't get a read on him at all. I didn't think of it at the time. He was just, like, empty."

"You need to find out about him," Dad says.

I call Susie from my cell. "Get in touch with Gordon's mom," I tell her.

"Why?"

"We need to know more about the kids in your tutoring class. Make up something, like you need some background to help create individual study plans."

"Dare I ask what this is about?"

"Maybe the reason I saw the black cloud around you first, before I dreamed about your mom and had a bad feeling about the group, is that it's someone *from* the group!"

"No way! They're in grade eight!"

"How much strength do you need to strangle some-one with their scarf?"

"Not much, I guess."

"I know it might be far-fetched, but I went to see that psychic guy at The Chocolate Shop. He used tarot cards to give me a reading and he saw numbers, he saw teenagers, and he saw you."

Pause.

"Susie?"

"I'll call her."

My brain is racing. Could it be one of those kids? And if so, how on earth are we going to prove it or get anyone to believe us?

I say that to Dad.

"One thing at a time," he answers. "Let's see what Susie can find out."

We're trapped in traffic at Confusion Corner when Susie calls back a few minutes later. "Here's what I could get out of her. Mindy is a dreamer, a good kid. She's brilliant at English, just doesn't get math. Justine is the opposite. She hates school. She gets the math, she just can't be bothered. She lives with her mom and dad, and has a younger brother who was sick with cancer but is in remission now. Chase, Gordon's younger brother, is having too much fun to study. And finally, Bob, the tall kid? She's not too sure about him. No mom in the picture, lives with his dad who has four other kids to take care of. She says the dad is not that forthcoming so she really can't tell me much."

"Bob," I repeat. "He's tall, so he'd be capable. And it fits with what John Smith told me. He said he felt a deep anger, so deep there were no clues, no *energy*, I think he said. And *I* couldn't get any kind of feeling from Bob. Now that I think about it, that's weird."

"But the police think they have the right guy," Susie says. "You'll never convince them."

"You're right," I agree. "I won't. So what do we do? Did you find out where Bob goes to school?"

"River Heights."

"I'll talk to my dad," I tell her, "and my mom. She can at least call Detective King and let him know. Meantime, don't let your mom out alone!"

"I'll try," she promises.

I turn to Dad. "We have an idea who it might be. But it's pure guesswork."

"Mom will call Detective King," Dad says. "We'll go from there." He pats my hand. "Head and heart. Logic and intuition. It's a good combination."

"I hope so," I say. I don't tell him, of course, but John Smith also said I might not survive this. No point going there.

THIRTEEN

Susie's mom has had enough. She says they've caught the guy and that's that. Detective King is sure they have him, and a few dreams aren't going to change his mind. But I can't leave it at that, so at lunch on Friday Susie and I discuss our options.

"I don't get it," I say. "My dreams led them to catch guy number one, so why are they saying now the dreams don't matter?"

"It's easier this way, I guess," she says. "They're just glad they have the guy, they did catch him in the act. Maybe it *is* all over."

"But can we take that chance?" I ask. "I mean, I hope more than anyone that it is over. And that this could just be a regular nightmare. But it didn't feel like that. Not at all."

Susie scowls. "I don't think we *can* take that chance. Which logically means that we need to track down our prime suspect."

"It's nice out today. Why don't we just walk past River Heights and see if we can find him? We can follow him, see if he's up to anything weird."

"How will we ever find him in that mob of kids?"

"True. Then we need to find out where he lives."

"I can do that," Susie says.

School drags all afternoon. But by end of class Susie has gotten Gordon to get Chase to find Bob's address —it's on the other side of the tracks. We need to go past River Heights on the way to his house, so we decide to walk instead of going by bus, just in case we do spot him.

We've been walking for a few minutes when Susie blurts out, "I feel bad for you."

"Huh?"

"You didn't ask for this and it's so weird, and it's so . . . ugly. I mean, why should you have to deal with all this? Dream about murders and murderers and stuff? It's not fair."

"My Baba says it actually runs in our family. I wonder if there could be some sort of genetic link," I muse. "Like gene mutation or something that lets people like me tune in. From those books you brought over it doesn't sound like something anyone studies for. I mean, they study and learn once they accept they have an ability, but they can't get rid of it." I sigh. "I tried."

"What did you do?"

"I took drugs this one shrink prescribed. They worked to a point but I was always in a kind of fog. My school work sucked."

"I remember," she says. "I thought it was just the after-effects of your meningitis."

"No, I was trying to get rid of all this. But then, when I was able to save those kids, I realized that, one, I could do some good, and two, it was useless to try to pretend it wasn't there. It's easier to accept it than fight it."

"Doesn't seem easy to me," Susie says.

"Well, maybe easy is the wrong word. But I mean, like, when did you finally accept you were going to be an egghead not a cheerleader?"

She thinks. "Must have been when we went into seventh grade," she says. "I'm getting almost perfect grades and getting teased like crazy for it. But I was proud of those grades. And," she adds, "I had you. And Jason."

"We weren't alone. That does make it easier," I agree.

Susie pats my back. "You aren't alone now either." Then she grabs my arm. "There he is!"

Sure enough. About a half block from us, heading down Grosvenor, is Bob. His blond hair and height make him stand out from the rest of the crowd walking home. At a mere minus ten no one has a hat on—lucky for us or we never would have spotted him.

"Now we follow him," I say.

~

"He looks so innocent," Susie comments as we walk, staying well behind him. "I can't imagine him hurting defenseless women. Why would someone do that?"

"Don't ask me!" I exclaim. "Ask my mom, she's the psychologist."

"Have *you* asked her?"

"Yeah."

"And?"

"I don't know. Lots of reasons. Tons of different reasons, a different one for each sicko, apparently. She does think that sometimes it's from lack of love, or shame. That kind of thing."

"It would be horrible to live in a home where no one loved you," Susie says.

"It would," I agree. "We're lucky. We can't even imagine how bad or horrible things must be to make a person want to lash out and kill someone. But do you know what bothers me? If there is some kind of universal plan and I fit into it, why does that plan have so much evil in it? I wish there was a plan that didn't have so much nasty."

Susie interrupts me, "Why is he turning down Ash? He lives over the tracks."

"Going to a friend's?" I say.

"Or going to my house," Susie says, the colour draining from her face.

I stop in my tracks. I look around. The day is sunny, just like in my dream. The light looks the same, too. And Bob is a full block and a half ahead of us now, because we were lagging as we talked, wanting to keep a good distance between us.

"Run!" I shout.

Susie and I sprint, but it isn't easy to move in a crowd of hundreds of seventh and eighth graders who purposefully take up space and won't move even if you're shouting.

And then I think—the phone. I yell to Susie, "Call your mom!"

She slows down a little, pulls out her cell, and speed dials. I'm ordering kids around us to get out of our way, occasionally pushing and shoving when they won't move on their own. Finally we turn onto Ash and stop. He's gone. Vanished. But Susie lives on the west side of the street, so if he were in the lane we wouldn't see him. We both have the same thought at the same time and race for the lane. Susie lives about halfway up the block. I don't see him. That's probably a bad thing.

"No answer," Susie says, stuffing the phone back in her jacket pocket as she runs. "She never answers her phone!" And then Susie's feet go out from under her, she slips on some ice, hitting the ground on her backside.

I hesitate for a moment. "Keep going!" she screams at me.

I do. I run, heart in my throat, dreading to see Bob standing over Susie's mom, scarf in his hand, his victim already dead.

Finally, finally, I get to their car port beside the garage and their gate. It's open a bit. It shouldn't be. If Mrs. Norman was carrying groceries, she would have gone into the yard straight from the garage. I push it open. And there they are. She's on the ground, just as I saw it, groceries everywhere. He's kneeling, pulling on her scarf, and I must fly from where I am because suddenly I'm on top of him and with my full weight I push him off Mrs. Norman. We land with a thud, him under me and for a moment neither of us moves. In the silence I can hear Susie's mom cough. The relief I feel when I hear that sound disappears as Bob throws me off him. He's strong. He whips the scarf off Mrs. Norman and scrambles up, holding it in front of him like a weapon. I can see he intends to use it on me. We're about the same height, but I'm still not at full strength, what with the meningitis and then the cold. He lunges for me and in an amazing move, somehow manages to wrap the scarf around my neck. I try to grab for him but he keeps dancing around me, all the time tightening the scarf. At least I've saved Susie's mom, I think, as I feel my throat tighten more and more. I desperately reach out, but spots are starting to blacken my vision and then, suddenly, I feel the scarf pull to one side and loosen. Out of the corner of my eye I see Susie deliver a kick to Bob's jaw. I hear it connect and I turn in time to see his head snap back. She kicks him again, this time in the chest, and then once more and he's flat on his back.

I pull the scarf off my neck and throw one end to Susie. She grabs it and we wrap it around his body so his arms are out of commission. Susie pulls out her cell and throws it to me as she bends over her mom. I dial 911.

Trouble is, I can't talk properly—my throat is all closed up—so I have to give it back to Susie. She pants out her address and asks for police and an ambulance. Her mom is still just lying there. She hit her head hard. But she's conscious. That has to be good.

Susie is asking me how I am. My head is spinning and my throat is tight but, hey, I'm okay. I'm alive. We all are.

Bob is starting to struggle up. Susie and I turn him onto his stomach and I sit on his back. He struggles and I'm worried he'll get loose but finally I hear sirens.

Soon two police arrive, a young man and an even younger woman. She handcuffs Bob and he checks Mrs. Norman. Then, the police woman asks me what happened. I tell her he's the scarf murderer.

She's about to object but I stop her. "I'm telling you, he's the one," I croak. "But careful with him. It's not just some teen punk you have there. Call Detective King."

As she does the ambulance arrives. The paramedics put Mrs. Norman on a stretcher and insist I come too and pretty soon we're all going downtown, Susie riding with us.

I lean back and finally hear Mrs. Norman speak. "Susie?"

"Yes, Mom, I'm here."

"Are you all right?"

"Yes."

"Jade? Is she all right?"

"We're fine," Susie assures her. "How are you?"

"The headache from hell," she cracks. "And my throat feels like it's been crushed, but I think I'm okay."

Susie is crying now. So I start to cry too.

But it's over. I can feel it. I can see it. The black cloud is gone. Gone.

It's over.

EPILOGUE

Mom, dad, and I are sitting in the living room. Marty is in bed. It's been a long night, what with getting checked at the hospital and answering questions at the police station. Detective King just called to say that I'd been right all along, the other guy was a copycat. This kid, Bob, told the police things only the true killer would have known, and it turns out the other guy actually had an alibi for the second killing.

"Do they know why Bob did it?" I ask.

"Only that his mom left the family when he was around eight and he never got over it. Dad wasn't cruel, just distant. Apparently, Bob heard voices telling him to do these things. I expect they'll find he's schizophrenic."

"Or just mad at his mom," I say.

Mom looks at me. "Or that."

"Do you think they'll ever know why those poor women had to die?" I ask.

"As a psychologist, I'll be the first to admit that at the core of every horrible action is a true mystery. Lots of kids lose their mothers, unfortunately. But what makes a kid like Bob do what he does? People have written books and articles but...."

"Okay," I say, "I get the mystery stuff—if anyone does I do—but why focus on Mrs. Norman when the others were just random?"

"Detective King says that when Bob saw her come pick you guys up something snapped. They think he was so jealous of Susie having a mom, a loving mom, that he fixated on her."

"But he was in the house of another nice mom— Gordon and Chase's mom. There are nice moms all over the place! Why Mrs. Norman?"

"Detective King says she looks remarkably like his own mom."

"Oh."

"Yeah, oh," Mom says.

"I don't know which is creepier, actually," I say. "Picking people to kill at random, just on a whim, or picking on someone for a 'reason,' but a reason that makes no sense."

"I think Susie would say that at least with him targeting her mom you were able to help," Dad says. "Those other poor women didn't have a chance." He pauses. "How is Susie handling all this?"

"She's cancelling her subscription to her skeptic magazine!"

He laughs. "Well, I can't say I blame her, but there are probably plenty of scams out there for her to debunk should she want to keep that up."

"I agree," I say. "I told her not to cancel. She says she doesn't want to be part of any 'belief' at all, including not believing in anything. Things are just too weird." I stop to think for a moment and then say, "But here's the thing: the first killings were random, and then he saw Susie and her mom and fixated on them. But I saw the dark cloud well before he met them. Logically, that would mean that this was all meant to be—everything, even the first murders and me saving the third woman and then Susie's mom almost dying."

"Almost dying," dad says. "That's the big word—almost. Because she didn't die. If she had, you might have said, well, it was meant to be—you saw the blackness, you predicted it. But it didn't happen that way, did it? Perhaps there are many, many timelines and each and every choice we make creates new ones, and then more new ones. And maybe some timelines are more likely to happen than others. But that doesn't mean that the less likely ones can't happen as well— sometimes."

The phone rings and Mom picks it up.

"It's Baba." She takes it to the kitchen and then comes back.

"I told Baba you'd call her tomorrow," she says. "She's invited us all to Palm Springs during spring break."

"But Dad can never go then," I say, not wanting to get my hopes up.

"Except I've been asked to speak at a conference in San Diego and have already agreed to go," Dad says.

"Really?"

"Really."

"So we're all going to Palm Springs in March?" And I remember that John told me this would happen.

"We are."

I'm so excited I can hardly stand it.

"We figure you could use a break," Mom says.

"Jon'll be disappointed," I say.

"He'll live," Dad grins.

"Yes," I say. Although I get a funny feeling as I say that. Never mind. I push it away.

The nightmares are over.

Two women saved.

Life is good.

For some reason, a line from *The Tempest* comes into my head.

"We are such stuff as dreams are made on; and our little life is rounded with a sleep."

Awake or asleep—which is more real?

Or are they actually *both* real—just different? And is it all magic? I may never know for sure. One thing I am sure of is that I'm lucky to have my best friend back. Whatever the truth is, we'll try to figure it out together.